The Gingko Tree and Other Poems

Palewell Press

The Gingko Tree and Other Poems

Michael Baron

The Gingko Tree and other poems

First edition 2023 from Palewell Press,
www.palewellpress.co.uk

Printed and bound in the UK

ISBN 978-1-911587-69-9

Cover design is Copyright © 2023 Kenneth Calhoun,
kennethjamescalhoun@gmail.com

Cover Photo by Benni Fish

The Gingko leaf images in the interior are Copyright ©
2023 Kenneth Calhoun

The back cover photo of Michael Baron is Copyright ©
2023 Saskia Baron

Setting by Amanda Helm, amandahelm@uwclub.net

A CIP catalogue record for this title is available from the
British Library.

Acknowledgements

Some of these poems have been published previously in: *Dreich, Other Poetry, South Bank Poetry, Jewish Quarterly, Morley College Magazine, The Third Way, The Journal, The Herne Hill Magazine*, and *Camden*.

Dedication

To all who have encouraged me, particularly my daughters, fellow poets, creative writing tutors, over the years with kind comments and hosts of thoughtful suggestions. It would be invidious to single anyone out by name. This little book is a great endeavour in which we have each played a part. Even the trees are players.

Contents

Preface

Looking over this collection, the first word that springs to my mind is "variety". Variety of subject matter, of shape, of pattern, of tone. This should not surprise; the poems are the fruits of a long life of rich experiences surveyed by an active, even restless, mind.

The second thing that strikes me is how personal the poems are. Whether the mood is elegiac, erotic, self-critical, or contemplative, they all reveal something about the self of the poet. This does not make them narrow or exclusive. Far from it; Michael Baron opens up private moments to connect with the reader. Human interconnectedness is his overarching theme.

The poems come from a lifetime's engagement with language, with the challenge of choosing and arranging words to form the best showcase for ideas. The influence of other poets is detectable – Wordsworth, Larkin, Norman Nicholson? – but Baron avoids pastiche or slavish imitation. His language is a fertile mix of the literary and the demotic. His scale of reference stretches from Virgil to Kilburn High Road.

There's a strong historical sense at work, too. The Kindertransport, National Service, radical politics in the Cold War period, political prisoners … the big subjects are interwoven with quotidian detail to bring them within the reader's range, to make us understand that history is made up of a myriad of actions and interactions. Baron often uses characters to encapsulate a historical moment – his Jewish migrant mother, a jailed Turkish poet, a cleaning lady, a refugee. Whether he sets his poem in London, Cumbria, Lithuania or Oregon, Baron shows us real human beings in real historical time, influenced by and having influence on their geographical and cultural surroundings.

The collection is unusual in showing an equal sensitivity to the natural and the built environment. Some of the most lyrical and tender poems use seasons, plants, trees and birds to express human emotions. The senses, and sense memories, are as important as – or more important than – Baron's ever-vigilant analytical intelligence. Emotions flow from the meeting of the conscious and the unconscious. These poems reveal that connection, and demonstrate, in their wonderfully various ways, that joy and grief, love and loss, are endlessly intertwined.

Charlotte Moore Writer and Journalist

Introduction

Some words in the form of an introduction about how one might read these poems. Some were written many years ago. At that time, I paid attention to punctuation. Later I concluded that it was a direction to the reader that he or she could do without. I have ideas about where to pause and be silent, where to breathe, where to be a bit of a performer, and so on. Some poems lend themselves naturally to stops and starts. Others need guidance or forethought. If one stops for sadness, the wistfulness of memory, the recollection of death, why should one not stop for a moment of joy? Ideas are personal.

So the later poems have little to guide the reader except a conclusive stop, sometimes a question mark or even nothing. Words often trail off into a world of silence where it is best to remain with the closing image which is also the last thought. Is a stop necessary? Maybe it is a sort of death each time. Now and then I have inserted brackets and dashes in a wilful attempt at a reference to another poem, as a tentative explanation of what the poem is trying to say. At other times I may refer to a person. Finally, those capital letters. In early poems each one may involve some enjambment so capital letters only follow full stops. In other poems I have begun each new line with a capital. That is only for the look on the page.

Is that important? But ultimately only the reader, whether alone or with listeners, is judge and jury of what can be a difficult question. How do I read this and where, if justified, do I pause, breathe or make some other gesture of empathy? Perhaps one's last words are in another language – *Chacun à son goût*!

Michael Baron 2023

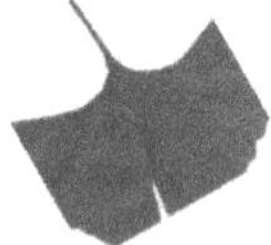

The Gingko Tree – The Meadow Burial Ground

You are taller now
than in our last encounter
gingko from China

tall among cypresses in the just cut grass.

That time we met you were entangled
with late summer's natives.

Today mid afternoon sun throws lingering shafts
to touch, then love

Your offshoot's branches at the topmost where
green leaves cling.

You are taller now than when I measured last

A yardstick I can reveal without tape or ladder.

Sure you'll outgrow us outpace

time and every human weakness.

Tree of the Ice Age
Taller now.

Mother (1897–1979)

If there is one thing that's truly certain
about you, painted at fifteen,
it is that you do not know your destiny.

Easy enough to find out how you began.
19, Lower Brunswick Street, the Leylands,
Leeds, one of hundreds, thousands, amongst
the huddled mass of migrants.

In the ambiguity of today a refugee.
Your Litvak parents speak a pungent mix of tongues.
Yiddish, a little Russian, poor English, Hebrew,
the last reserved for prayers on Sabbath.

And you. How were you
Tsvi (meaning 'gazelle')
Ha-Levi's grand-daughter
picked out to be the doctor
you will become? High school,
scholar, then university.
The road south is open wide.
Spells ambition, sacrifice.

It made you different, girl of rouged cheeks
painted in the white regulation blouse,
neat bow tie, long hair to the waist.
I sense you were never quite convinced

you were one of them. Who is? You stare
from the scuffed frame, on the doubtful edge
of another life, and let imagination
transport to places you dreamed of.

Dreamed standing upright now in Chapeltown,
a young woman, painter unknown, for whom
Homer, Sophocles, Ovid were intimate as home.
For you, we light *jahrzeit*, watch it flicker,
like a baby's breath, a fitful flame, every year.

Flowers Without Words

In long
Unruly hedgerows
In crevices of old stone walls
Piled high on top of coffins and shimmer wrapped
On Sheraton sideboards in second homes
For the sighted the transitoriness of life
For the almost blind the smell the smell
The pointer of snowdrops clutch
To winters soil the first green flags
The wet beginning of new days
The lonely patch of frost on the field
Flowers by crosses at uncared for rural cenotaphs
In empty lanes commons corners alleys
Between lovers exchanging last embraces
Between mourners head bare overcoated
The open grave
Flowers without words

Not The End of the Dance

Sometimes I sense I have come to the end
to the end of my dance be it two step
or three or waltz or a lovely jig round rooms
and kitchens and yards sometimes real
sometimes in dreams

Sometimes in dreams I twirl you around
rooms and kitchens where the floors
are made for dances that will never end
will go on for hours if not a hundred years
in each other's arms

In each other's arms we'll kiss now
and kiss again and be content
smiling and joking not being
angry not being somewhere else
not being far away

Not being far away is what I want
and maybe you too and not for
the dance to end but to go on
as long as there is music a parquet floor
to try two steps or waltzes or just twirls

Two steps or waltzes or just twirls
to jig around rooms and kitchens
and yards sometimes real
sometimes in dreams

Mornings in South Street

White blind and open window,
The mornings in South Street.

Where are you, in what autumn now,
In what high atrium of the afternoon?

A thrush displays a speckled
Breast, and a blackbird lights on
The earth softly as paradise.
Picking diffidently a brown apple
Rolled in the grass
Disturbed by half a dozen
Sparrows on the morning call
To feeder, nuts and grain, eating
Like starvation was another kingdom,
And a coal tit is looking in, while,
Late, the blue headed one hops
Down from conifer hedge to see what
Is going on here now food is all about,
Which ushers in the dovenish pair,
Black collar necklaces, jumping
Branch to branch in athletic leaps.

You, too, would hop, jump, and leap.
Your flesh remembered.
Where are you, in what autumn now,
In what high atrium of the afternoon?

The mornings in South Street,
White blind and raised window.

Cathedral

I light two candles
In the cathedral of Coutances.
One is for you.
I used to watch the slow burn taper touch
Slim wax candles
And never asked *for whom?*
For God? For those you loved?

In churches we visited,
Your candles lit up the dark
– Aisle, arch, corner, apse –
So many times, so many times.
On white stems like flowers,
Two flames grew and grew
Joining others in a bright array.
Such acts, worship, homage,
Wishful thought, prayer, old memory –
You did often. For this was where
Each visit to Gothic or Baroque began.
I light two. I think I'll do that
For ever.

      One for you, one for me,
Making these moments,
This   this illumination   ours.

Call Me

Call me before leaving
Kiss me before dying

Turn round at the station
As you mount the train

Look me straight in the eye
Let me touch your cheek

I have packed your bags
One skirt and a blouse

One dress and fine shoes
I have handled them all

I know how you dressed for work
How you undressed for bed

I'm sad that you're going
And sad that I'm staying

So call me before leaving
Kiss me before dying

Thurlestone Church

Usually I had no words
or had used them up
after porridge
and coffee had been consumed.
You said nothing until late,
might be noon, when I tired
of talking to eccentric drivers
or helloing carelessly from lorries.
Between lifts we wallowed in the grass
like half-awake insects, awaiting
the big one, none came, no great wave, just a car.

And now I stand, somewhat Lutheran,
By the church door – dark inside, and
your coffin just here.
I'm about to tell all I know of you.
Did you believe in Him?
The vicar, watching what his flock did or did not do,
While I could only think of your absence there.

I put my fingers on the wood,
your container now, recited
Eliot – the steps down to the rose garden,
the lotus (was it?) rising, the blackbirds
in the shrubbery and children's voices –

how the congregation listened, letting time move
between then and now, past and present,
before the coffin was moved off its stand.

Jim, you're gathered up, you're nearly gone.
I followed wife, now widow, mother, children,
to the allotted place, near your father.
The last time I walked slow between the stones,
you were there amongst the flowers,
silent among the bright leaves of summer.

Swimmer

For Ilhan Sami Çomak: Sillivri Prison, Turkey

There is warm weather today.
He writes from prison saying
He does not know Wordsworth
But that moving from reading
To writing is his necessity if
The spirit is to stay alive.

How does the spirit stay alive
When early flowers grow beyond
The bars and in the mountain villages
Snowdrops gather in clusters
Free and unashamed?

He does not think he deserves
The title 'poet' more a teller
Of tales a chronicler it's more
Important to be human open
Loosed from evil nothingness.

He is a swimmer who has to swim
Because he is in the sea
Because each wave threatens
Because wild currents will move
Him too quickly from the land.

Swimming is what a man does
A moving body is rhythm
Hands arms and legs together
Bright breath dreams its way
Eyes fixed unblinking on safe blue hills.

He writes daily from prison
Like the bravest of men
He'll reach the fabled shore of love
But when when when
Even as long seasons drift and teach.

Meeting with a Refugee

He stood there tall and single at the corner of the street.
His T-shirt ripped, brown skin scratched and scarred.
His feet not in sandals but Oxford brogues, polished, neat.
A kindly driver had put him down. The pavement's hard,

but did for sleep. "*Inshallah*" he intoned "at last, I'm here."
The leaking boat, the sea, rescue, walk, fenced border, train.
Often on the journey, loss, loneness, despair, were near.
The stamp, the safe escape, asylum grant, erased the pain.

I was moved to touch one bare arm and say "hello",
ask about his shoes, boast how others would provide,
somewhere in a city would be rooms to rent, fellow
men who could find him work, yet something in me died.

Was I the Other, the enemy, the cynic, exhausted, worn
down, photos of carnage, murder? Did I have time?
Strange friend – I think he said – *here is no cause to mourn.*
None – I was, for one moment, the Other –
save the undone years.

All poets share. We've read our Wilfred Owen.
War we sort of know. Beheaded men,
kids with guns and rubble. And me, old observer,
cushioned watcher of indifferent times?
I knew shame's pay-back that kindness spelt trouble.

I am ashamed. I left him single, alone, at the corner
of the street. Raised high our ungrasped hands,
said farewell, and went our separate roads,
potholed as the desert to meet our ends.
The unshared years, ruins, bombs, the dreams, the lies.

Ponary, Lithuania, 2005

On State Bank notes, poets and pilots.

In woods at the road's end
some metres beyond a bridge
arched over marshalling yards,
past sagging fences and cottages,
a woman pointed the way
to our driver, who resembled
Josef Stalin, but younger,
and spoke no Russian,
to the Memorial.

In woods at the road's end.
Incised elegantly in Cyrillic
recording for us, visitors,
Jews who asked the way
of an old woman at a cottage door
to the massacred
'Victims of Fascism.'

It was not summer any more
in the woods at the road's end
and outside sagging cottages
timber lay piled against winter.
Easy to feel cold standing
in my Hugo Boss overcoat.

After all, this was October,
trees yellowing like stars –
which is the wrong image but
you'll know what I mean.

Leaves were slowly skirling down,
sunlight picking out skeletal trees,
as if nothing had ever happened,
as if the mounds and ditches
and the pit I could have fallen into
had never been dug, dark earth
never piled up to conceal
massacres of seventy thousand.

We came by taxi on a highway
that wound through a forest
and were quite alone,
not speaking, not to the driver
who resembled Josef Stalin, but younger,
not to each other, thinking this is one
hell of a way to walk from the city
carrying a suitcase and a child in tow
past the shocked grandmother of a woman,
her jumper torn.

/continued

At that time timber would not have
propped up the sagging fences,
there would have been flowers
at painted front doors, in vases
on sills behind drawn curtains.
And railway trucks being shifted
skilfully in the marshalling yards
coupling to long-distance trains.
Perhaps there were no trees
nor any wood at the road's end,
but open heath, a wide clearing,
making it easy to dig ditches, pits,
pile up dark earth in mounds,
without a memorial in elegant Cyrillic
for happy boys on bicycles to ride round
whooping when we were near crying.

No poets, pilots,
Just two boys on bicycles.

When He Was Five

When he was five, each night
he said his prayers. Mickey was
a Mouse, Popeye ate spinach,
fairies hid at the long garden's end.

And when he was six, his father
told him to read 'How We Began' –
silent stirrings of intertidal slime
convinced his open mind.

No God. Nature, Tennyson said, was
'*red in tooth and claw*'. Darwin, too.
No more is needed for unbelief.
Let's search skies for the Pleiades.

Kindertransport 1938

Some clutched teddy bears
some held suitcases
were dressed for outings
wore their best clothes
said *auf wiedersehen* to *sacher torte*
Wiener schnitzel gefilte fisch
and all the *gemütlichkeit*
of well-furnished rooms
lives of utmost regularity

Some one day were reunited
others never saw Mama or Papa
again and held for ever a picture
of the great Berlin *hauptbahnhof*
and parents dressed for Shabbat
they were not going on holiday
to St Moritz Meiningen or Ettersberg,
but on a journey of re-creation –
Max to Martin, Helga to Henrietta Smith.

Older ones might have gone back
to *Heimat, Marktplatz* (once paraded
on *Krystallnacht* by mayoral *diktat*)
wearing khaki, two stripes, a single pip
and given orders to frightened clerks.

Most never talked of seeing fathers,
grandfathers, scrub shit from pavements
some in the faded uniform of the Kaiser
oh memories are sepia snaps with holes
like favoured sweaters worn
after visitation of the moth.

> *Is there ever a best time to remember*
> *I didn't hear you repeat it slowly please*
> *after me that's it but*
> *what was that you said*
> *I didn't hear you*

Second-hand Silence

They doused seven candles to touch darkness
inside and out, stood overcoated, the family group,
as if a local photographer with lens and hood
waited by some garden gate for the final snap,
but waiting were lorries, murmur of engines
exhaling slow drifts of smoke in side streets,
and more rebuffs to silence, the voices;
children's voices, shrill, quickly subdued,
asking why candelabra lay under snowdrops
beside plate, sports cups, the Great War sword,
Iron Cross for bravery at the Front, why Hansi
had been put down, cats left to stray, hunting
for rats; and neighbours drew curtains, argued
later, picked locked doors, self-help to what
couldn't be packed into one case per person
and bedding rolls as the youngest bemused how
at midnight mother wears best dress, fur tippet,
muff, father a favourite suit, with newish fedora.

So where's the microphone to overhear slam
of tail-boards, howl of abandoned animals, footfall,
lorries in side streets, the usual cool South wind which,
another night, fought to bend and break
silver birches on the lakeshore, disturb water
near a villa fierce with light, as plans were made
between cigars, the best cognac, the finest glass.

No, none of this was recorded by newsmen, caught
in the scratchy far-offness of film reels and yet,
forever second-hand, absent, users of what isn't ours,
obsessed, puzzled, students of memorials and memorabilia,
we'll never see what they saw, nor have to still
voices of children, faced with unknowing,
but instead wrestle with the sense of this:

    'I would like to write and remain silent.'

A Classical Education

It was the smell in bare corridors,
the bygones of collegiate cooking,
old cabbage, potato, cheese, and sweat.
Small boys who hated washing hands
and missed their mums like hell.
This was education, paid for.
This was learning, where damp
mornings started with prayers
in Latin – the founder four centuries
before decreed and she must be obeyed –
Oremus and then *pater noster*
We learnt that patter quickly.

The headmaster was J. T. Christie.
A 'J' much more like 'Jesus' when
he took a class, at Buckenhill,
rebuked Smith or Jones for daring to respond –
hoc magister.
We laughed too, quick, respectful.
After all, he was HM, knew our names,
would add a note in term reports.
Told us in church that 'sex,' yes, sex,
'was a great and beautiful thing'.
Which we knew well, lusting after maids
and Mrs Murray-Rust on Sundays.

You don't forget the Latin
even though sex was deemed to
disappear after long cross-country
runs through heather, gorse, rain or dry,
the Bringsty miles, endless slog, once a week.
We could still spot hexameters in verse,
Greek or Latin; this was learning, paid for.
Textbooks had owners, scrawled, smudged,
names of the dead in read out school litanies
The next goodbyes for us? Might it be over

before *Ire licet* – you're free to go? Free to go –
to war, where each noun has four letters,
and future tenses can't explain, nor Virgil
instruct how, the stripping down of guns,
polish on boots, a belt's brass buckles, Blanco,
leads to endings, roadside, ditch, elsewhere.

Talking to Shostakovich

and other Russians was
always my ambition though
I did not rule out Stalin, if he'd
listen. Certainly, I missed deep
conversations on revolution with Trotsky

since the ice-pick beat me to it
one August afternoon in Mexico.
He, the Generalissimo, preferred,
I guess, to talk of the Terror,
a famine in Ukraine, show trials
of enemies, Siberia, exile
to the gulag of Mandelstam,
indicting Babel, harassment of Tsvetaeva
for poems in praise of White Russians.

We could have chatted, Stalin and me, of the old days,
bank raids in Baku,
grape quality in Georgia,
how to make a bomb that worked,
that poem he wrote 'To The Moon'.
I settled for power
the facts inside the red jackets of the Left Book Club –
'Fallen Bastions', 'Red Star Over China',
Koestler's 'Spanish Testament',
papered over deaths.

So I toured, by bus, the run-down Hackney halls,
sometimes Cricklewood, off Shoot Up Hill.
My raging nights were there, young radical,
among bentwood chairs, sagging platforms
which by day had kids acting *Mother Goose,*
at Christmas *Aladdin* or *Sleeping Beauty.*
Nights were for Harold Laski, suited,
spectacled, exhorting us to storm Whitehall,
egged on by Kingsley Martin, his white hair
dishevelled as his trousers – boy, was he angry,

wild with Churchill, the army, General Scobie
for interfering the old way which
Greeks did not like after losing Smyrna
25 years before, and Seferis writing
'the houses that I had they took away from me.'
but the Russians, oh the Russians,
I never got to talk to any ever,
not even Shostakovich and now he's gone
yet that Eighth Quartet – *wow.*

The Happening

The boys swam in the river
While older brothers and sisters
Helped with the plough or milking,
Stripping feathers off chickens
Before the feast, and if
The mood came on them hiding
In the densest part of the field
Where the wheat was as high as
The eaves of houses, making love
Before time for marriage and procreation.
Growing up meant being tested.
With spears or arrows to fell a man,
Make enemies dead, though they asked
Several times *what is an enemy?*
Until that evening, coming back late
From hunting wild boar,
The bright bronze of armoured men,
Catching smell of horses
(which none of their families owned).

Too late to run away, disappear
In a far field, where the wheat is high,
From the chief whose breast plate
Was the sun who said

There was a big war over the sea,
In a place called Troy, Achaeans
From Sparta, Thebes, far-off Crete,
Had to muster, serve Agamemnon.

The king had summoned judges, commanders,
Priests, wise men and shipmasters
To his many-roomed palace at Argos,
Told them that the gods wanted this,
Not least Athena. What she said went,
One did not disobey gods lightly.
So all of us who'd thrown a spear,
Brought down a deer at fifty paces
With an arrow clean to the heart,
What could we do but volunteer?
Mothers howled most horribly
In front of girlfriends, who knew
Weddings would not happen, nor babies
Proud on shoulders, for several years,
Or maybe never. Protesilaus,
Who knew more than most,
Muttered about Thanatos and Hypnos.
We did not stay to wonder
But rushed back to stammer farewells,
Gather up clothes, unused weapons.

You ask me now. That was how it happened.

Missing the War

We missed it. We were too young.
Could never say, with conviction,
That hard to believe, *I had a good war.*

His might not have been so good.
There were others, small, lesser ones,
Palestine, Korea, communist Malaya.

He was too young but marched in step
up and down, down and up, in unison
on snowy barrack squares of Surrey.

Stupid wars like Suez, but his Lee-Enfield
was stripped in classrooms, lugged impressively
with maps around country signposts

and village shops. In chilly three-ton lorries,
bored conscripts in baggy khaki defended
Aldershot, died each week for King and Country.

Really it was for acned subalterns they died,
for sergeant majors who excelled at shouting
'You liquid streak of piss' at sloping shoulders,

Yet earned big respect for insights learned
in bombed Cologne, back streets of Amsterdam,
the strange ways of women, their pliant bodies.

They missed it. They were simply too young.
And me, well, I don't cry for men I bayoneted
made of sack and straw, bloodless, silent

as the eight-inch blade slipped in, twisted, in
then out as if greased by Sainsbury's butter.
For afters there was tea with sticky buns.

One man's mug saw two years of service.
But we were lucky, didn't have that war.
Our names were not etched on cenotaphs

to be saluted, wept for, as the Last Post
sounds Remembrance Day in Whitehall.
We were just too young. We missed it.

Bone and Wood

Bone, wood, metal, plastic.
Bobbins are historic, rounded,
Domestic. The Singer whirring
In the day nursery, my mother
On the treadle, the machine,
Black and gold, was Engineering
In the home – dresses, napkins, hankies.

Our bobbins came from B. B. Evans
Far down the Kilburn High Road,
Department store to the middle class
Who shopped for fruit and veg at
Cluttered stalls where hoarse
Men, white-scarved, shouted about *ripe*
Tomatoes, Fyffes bananas, spuds,
Cauliflowers big as Mrs Gater's breasts.

She said her George (from Lancashire),
He'd gawn a lad from workhouse to mill
In the bobbin trade. And *it were rough …*
I saw sawdust, shavings, a bobbin maker
Among the flapping belts, the noise.
He slipped and lost 'is arm.
The cutter took it orf.
He sits at 'ome, coughs –it's 'ard.

The pinafore Mrs Gater wore
To clean, and never changed,
Was flowered – for years it hung
Behind the yellow cupboard door.
The lino floor she swept with rage
As if it were that Lancashire mill.
It was the birch wood they used,
He said, so wet, and sappy, loose.
She found my toy, my bobbin,
A danger which she threw away.

Powell's Bookshop, Portland, Oregon

The last Saturday of May.
Across the street without
Entering, the Buffalo Exchange bar
Proclaims in letters only the blind
could not read, WE ARE HIRING –
APPLY IN STORE TODAY. I don't.
For at the plain table in Powell's
Coffee room among the books and mugs
Arnold Drake World, his name, black, handsome
Is making extraordinary paper sculpture.
Flowers in vase, subtle leaf and blossom.
He twirls and twist. Strips of tissue
Float from his hands in the electric air
As I ask Arnold Drake World how and why.
He says his creations are derived from mathematics,
Assumes I know everything about the Fibonacci
Sequence, so I lie knowingly, not to disturb his fingers
As they work, his shoulders swaying to music
In his ear plugs, eyes on the paper in clever hands
Not on the hanging sign over our heads:

Coffee 400–409
Erotica 411–412
Graphic novels 401–402
Romance 406–412

Romance and erotica, six shelves of kiss and tickle
Brought me here to floors and floors of books,
It keeps me here while Portland comes alive
In the casual strolling on sidewalks, the ringing
Of tramcar bells, the slow European ease of Saturday,
Pop-up Vietnamese food stalls, silent construction sites,
Homelessness, a smell of grass,
but this is Powell's City of Books on Burnside,
every day full of eager buyers and Cherokees
whose literary adventure in pine studded woods
fill a million shelves.

I am reading the new Mary Oliver, and found
Nissim Hikmet while Arnold Drake World
from Wisconsin throws his wisps of paper,
Easy once you know how, he says,
Twisting between his fingers slivers of blue
Grow into rose petals or buds as Fibonacci has his
Way, in time for Arnold's TV show tomorrow afternoon.
Here the oversupply of polystyrene mugs
Doubles up as antique vases at no cost at all.
Coffee's getting real cool, I say from observation
Of Arnold Drake World's flowers, best to be found
In Powell's Books on the last Saturday of May.

The Message – 1952

It was on his desk at close of day
Like a tardy welcome mat
Or the postman's special delivery.
The paper pink, the message typed
On the large Adler in the back room,
Why don't you look at me?

Some days she would add *ever*,
Knowing his speaking look was *never*.
Sometimes, it's true, she dipped
Her middle finger in the inkwell
And scrawled, when he was out,
On the grimed window as if she

Played Miss Froy in 'The Lady Vanishes'.
But she did not. She was Doreen
In Typing, within a hand's reach of 40
Or so it seemed to him who'd
Just begun to shave and dream
Of ladies in see-through underwear.

If the line had been from Wordsworth,
Donne, Horace, or favoured Catullus,
He might have taken note,
Wondered about marching into
Typing and saying, blush emergent,
Doreen, are you free tonight?

Perhaps next week you're OK for lunch –
Lyons Corner House, the ABC,
The sandwich bar, they're quick…
He didn't. Her Adler emasculated men.
Besides, behind dark glasses, who was she?
A bed-sit in Hampstead, Norwood or Anerley?

Doreen in Typing would never know
He wanted this (and much else) on his pad
Give me a thousand kisses, a hundred more
another thousand and another hundred …
Or if Latin, not Pitman's, was her strength
Da mi basia mille, deinde centum,

deinde mille altera, deinde secunda centum…
This was an office without frontiers.
No centurion marched its dusty floors
Policing romance, destroying notes.
Doreen, well, she'd write the same to
young men, until she retired.

He who loved hendecasyllabics, not girls,
Is a judge, the river at his gate,
Walks quiet alleys while tower block LEDs
Are dimmed, extinguished. Such late nights
Encourage strange fantasies of what
He missed, wanting Latin not English invitations.

One Might

One might start,
Nervously,
With jasmine, flowers,
Taste of sherbet,
Pungent pomegranate
By desert pools, some oasis
Amongst the dunes.
But it would be wrong.

More like coal dust,
The dark sweat
Of nanny's armpits,
The gardener's earthy
Odours as he sat sipping,
In yesterday's old clothes,
Tea at the kitchen table
Where they cleaned the silver.

Apple Tree

Monday the apple tree
Is at the door.
Christmas Pippin,
Wrapped tight from
Its Cornish journey
Ready for earth
And spring and blossom's
Return to fruit

And this morning
The bedwarm of you
Next me, you are earth
It is Spring and blossom until
Alarms push you up
And out into the cold.
I do not know how lovely
You are until you close

The door to leave me with
My apple tree as
Ransom for your return.

At the Villa Diodati near Lausanne – June 1816

Shelley is sitting in the dark.
Mary he can hardly see.
Tallow candles are so dim.
In bed, night-shirted clutching the other
They talk of ghosts, mania, madness.

But sleep their separate nightmares.
Hers that he left her.
Went sailing.
Capsized to drown a mile off Lerici.

His that she was famous,
Reinventing a body
That made her gothic.

Epiphany of a Plantsman

I planted every sapling. The ground was good each time.
My hands were strong, dirt under fingernails
Was black. I loved delving in mud, getting the mix
Of sand to soil just right. Make them windfast, firm.
Each to celebrate a birth and when I passed the house
Last week, paint peeling off sills, each was a tree.

My God, trees! Lit up in fire, the stem's shine
Climb high minute to minute as, surprised,
A squirrel leaps, branch to branch, ruddered
By the brush of tail; the beast knew joy.
I don't have much of that now. No one calls.
The bike rusts, the spade's blunt, cycle clips hold bills

I cannot pay. But if I could plant trees again,
Pretend I am Tradescant or the capable Brown,
Workmen to order, a thousand trees, a ducal wood,
Rivers to divert to lake and waterfall; I'd be expert.
Long landscapes, summer's dream horizons, scented nights
Are ravaged, gone.
                    Where is my *garden of earthly delights?*

The Tree

She paints the tree
as she has always done
in the colour of rainbows.
Branches with a hogs hair brush,
twigs specks of burnt sienna,
leaves stabs of Hooker's Green,
slicked in by a palette knife,
sharp as an executioner's blade.

Let it dry, close the door on it,
left quietly on slim bare feet
the way a clandestine lover goes.
Overnight, alone, calmly content,
she dreamed top soil, compost,
the sexy in-and-out slow worm slither.

Waking sated, smelt broken clays,
earth's crumbling clods, opened curtains
to a gilded morning, turned the key,
the door rustling into a garden,
a tree heavy and rich with blossom.
Boughs bent with it, widespread with it,
spilling out of windows over the street.

All day people filled baskets with petals,
over breakfast, lunch, tea told their children
who told their friends who told theirs.
When night knocked like a shy policeman,
the tree surrendered, pleaded guilty,
defenceless, tired from fecundity,
such a fierce wild lust to be alive.

Became reluctantly an ordinary thing, flat,
another paint-laden canvas,
hoisted on a cheap easel for viewing,
possession, desire, 'my dear, how much?'

She had painted a tree
as she had always done.

Sensuality – Gaza – August 2014

I have heard of the smell of death
sometimes glanced nervously
as if not wanting to be seen,
glancing at photographs, news,
items of evidence of the dead,
though really evidence of being –
shoes, leather laces awry, decomposing –
and as I look and look away –
we do both, don't we? I think
of men and women and children
too many each of us, each of us,
a sprawled manky donkey
just when the last shell caught
before the cease-fire, before the truce,
caught unaware, caught
unaware and in every unhappy
irredeemable death-note I use these
words more than once, there is
an unusual still sweetness that's
new, moving shamefully, strangely,
out of the dream which holds me
into the rubble of a street, strewn plaster,
dust, paper, more staining, dirt nothing
will wash away and then into a cleaner
place, rubble this time of stones,

a purer place, boulders scattered, not
yesterday but over millennia, between
one end of a worn path and the top
of a mountain which is not here,
never will be here. And if, and if
we could each of us, the viewers,
smell, be alone just for a moment
in the ruins that will never be archaeology,
will be its twin angry brother, history,
and its bastard unloved son, politics,
for that moment each of us could be
the sprawled donkey, or better (better?)
the owner who lived next door, who saw
nothing except tumbled concrete walked
with a stick, with care, and then there was
silence, we might upon reflection,
do things differently, so that there are
no photographs, no news items, to read,
nervously wonder what death truly smells
like, and why aren't there shoes on ordinary feet
on the pavements of busy streets.

How is it that you live,
and what is it that you do?

(Wordsworth – Resolution and Independence)

He brought his findings to the Institute,
Tooting Common man, Herne Hill's batologist.
His beard, entangled round a jaw impossible to
discover, the baggy breeches familiar, as
was his turn-of-century stovepipe hat.
On days of rain or thin London sun he'd
mount the seven steps, white-scrubbed then,
to ring the bell. Sometimes my turn
at answering and he was there with
a leather bag – *Mornin' young man.*
I was 50 at the time, I laughed.
Here's more of them brambles,
I had a grand day, yesterday, movin'
– (saying *grand day* like a man
of Cumberland would on a fell top) – *movin'*
from bush to bush, florets
coming out, surprised like, little
charmers. So I looked and picked
a few stalks. You ain't seen these
before, that is, I am the only one
who knows the Common as if I
were raised there. He pushed past,
walking slowly, he'd aged since

I last met him talking
to himself, scratched bag held so
tight – his reddened scarred arthritic
hand – stopped at the door.
I heard Arthur call, *Hallo, Tom –*
got some more of the buggers for me,
Have you?… You have, oh that's good.
I guess that's eighteen now, maybe
they should name it Bramble Common
a shade more meaningful than Tooting.

I let Tom out, the bag empty, and
by the door he stopped, turned round,
I don't reckon I'll be here again
so dry 'em, frame 'em well, they'll
be my, what's the word, epitaph.
With a clique of mates, he's gone.
I think often of blackbirds picking at the fruit,
sharp taste of berry ceding place to song.

Hello Autumn

Hello, Autumn. My urban morning for small leaves
on pavements, for the late breeze turning on the tree,
for joyous smiling lovers, for *Halloo, come in*, buy
the latest thing in breads, indulge the barista grin.

Hello, Autumn. How travelled cases clatter click
the upward mobile streets from Paddington and – *look
at the guide* he says (overheard) *the listed bawdy
House*. Oh yes, it's been Autumn here since 1856.

Heigh-ho. The sere and faded yellow petals post licked,
stuck on York stone flags, tell – *oh baby mine – it's time,
it's really time to go*, we are shutting way down the line
those territories once we occupied, and now disdain.

So, who wrote *it was closing time in the gardens*
and added *of the West?* Moment of an August night,
our First World War when chandeliers were dimmed,
lamps out in Europe, then almost everywhere.

Hello, Autumn. And goodbye. Loved you not enough.
Softness, rot, decay, your hoarse tubercular breath,
your remorseless clock ding-donging darker evenings,
the measured silent wail of flowers, end-game of beauty
in doomsday loneliness, the lost rococo hours.

The Gingko Tree – Cockermouth

Dieses Baumes Blatt, der van Osten …

In Weimar, Goethe's loved tree grows splendid
By his planked *gartenhaus* October will
turn sunward a grand host of golden leaves.
Ancient perennial, the message is millennia,
ice, time, age; your short knobby branches

bare in winter, await the burst of spring,
fan-shaped, green, tip-crowded, unusual.
I planted *Ginkgo biloba* on the grave,
nursed by death, north light, wind,
her *Lied von der Erde* is Cumberland.
Each visit sings a different song.

A sprig, come in a shopper's paper bag,
air-travelled, snuggled from Thuringia,
I could imagine, was sprung from his,
took root, is resolute, a foreign field
becomes English; square patch of England.
I watched the thing growing, you beneath.

/continued

I told McTavish, keeper of the ground,
it's an oak, rare, modest, not high,
native like ash or white-skinned birch.
Duty made me lie. Homeland's a distance,
Tianmushan, streams, grassy banks, rock.
Tree, grow tall like love;
no oak was thus.
This tree's leaf, from the East…

Notes

'The Gingko Tree', p. 5. The Gingko tree comes from Weimar where Goethe lived and was imported from China where it is a native tree, pre-dating the Ice Age.

'Mother – 1897–1979', p. 6. *Jahrzeit* is the memorial candle observant Jews light on the anniversary of the death of a relative and which burns throughout the day of remembrance. My mother, whose portrait as a young woman is shown below, was born in 1897 in the Leylands, an area of Leeds heavily populated by immigrants from Eastern Europe.

'Mornings in South Street', p. 10. 'Dovenish' refers to the Yiddish habit of saying prayers and moving the whole body at the same time.

'Thurlestone Church', p. 14. This poem was written after several visits to the church at Thurlestone where I had spoken at the funerals of my Cambridge friend, James (Jim) Henry Prowse, and his mother and his sister. The family had lived in the village.

'Cathedral', p. 12. Coutances is a town in Normandy with a medieval cathedral.

'Swimmer', pp. 16. Written in 2014 for the imprisoned Ilhan Sami Çomak who found writing poetry to be his vocation. In 1994 Çomak was studying at Istanbul University when he was sentenced, wrongly, to 36 years in prison for terrorism and membership of the banned KKP (Kurdish Workers Party). He has been in prison since he was 22 years old, Turkey's longest serving political prisoner. He won the Sennur Sezer prize for his 'Geldim Sana' in 2019, and the Metin Altiak Award in 2021 for his 'Hayattayiz Nihayet'. Only these last two collections are available in print, with his autobiography *Karinca Yuvasini*. A selection of his poems translated into English and edited by Caroline Stockford has been published by Smokestack Books. And in 2023 a comprehensive selection from all his collections will be published in Turkey. In 2024 another collection of new poems will appear.

'Meeting with a Refugee', pp. 18. The quotations are from 'Strange Meeting', the poem by Wilfred Owen in 1918.

'Ponary, Lithuania, 2005', p. 20. Ponary or Paneyri is an area of woodland some ten miles west of Vilna in Lithuania. It was a killing place during the Holocaust. Before the collapse of the Soviet Union, the memorials displayed at the site commemorated 'Victims of Fascism' and claimed Ponary as a site where Soviet citizens were massacred. It was not until recently that it was acknowledged that around 75,000 Polish and Lithuanian Jewish citizens from Vilna, Kaunas and other cities had been brought to Ponary to be murdered.

I was aware that the overcoat I wore that day was made by Hugo Boss, Hitler's favourite tailor. During the war, the Hugo Boss company produced uniforms for the SS, SA and Wehrmacht.

'Kindertransport', p.24. The imagined conversation is with a resident in a home for the aged. The towns, Meiningen and Ettersheim, are near Weimar; one has a famous theatre, and the other a palace where Goethe once acted. Weimar is only five miles from Buchenwald concentration camp.

'Second-hand Silence', p. 26. The quotation which ends the poem is a line from the Catholic Hungarian poet, János Pilinszky (1921–81). The villa 'fierce with light' is the Wannsee villa where the Nazi leaders developed the so-called 'Final Solution'.

'A Classical Education', p. 28. At Westminster School, not only did the Headmaster end his lessons with the Latin phrase, but used the Elizabethan pronunciation as allowed by Queen Elizabeth I.

'**Talking to Shostakovich**', p. 30. 1945 was a year of civil war in Greece and much public agitation. George Seferis, born in Smyrna in modern Turkey, is the significant Greek poet of the century and a Nobel Prize winner for his contribution to world literature. Harold Laski was a Marxist professor at the LSE, and Kingsley Martin was the then editor of the *New Statesman*.

'**The Happening**', p. 32. Hypnos and Thanatos were the twin gods of sleep and death in Greek mythology. Protesilaus was the heroic leader of the Greeks who fell at Troy.

'**Bone and Wood**' p. 36. Mrs Gater was the daily help at 56 Chatsworth Road, NW2. My version of London slang is just that – a version.

'**The Message – 1952**', p. 40. The quotations are from *Springing from Catullus* (Catullus' *Carmina:* 'Vivamus mea Lesbia atque amemus') in the translation by Christopher Pilling, published by Flambard Press in 2009.

'**Epiphany of a Plantsman**', p. 45. The Tradescants, father and son, were the pre-eminent gardeners and plant hunters of the 17th century. The father's cabinet of curiosities is reputed to be the nucleus of the Ashmolean Museum in Oxford. *The Garden of Earthly Delights* is the title of the famous triptych by Hieronymus Bosch of 1590, in the Prado Museum, Madrid.

'**How is it that you live, and what is it that you do? – Tooting Common Man**' p. 50. If the reader has the time, visit the South London Botanical Institute at 323 Norwood

Road, SE24. It is an unusual small museum, devoted to plant specimens.

'The Gingko Tree – Cockermouth', p. 53. The opening quotation in German is the first line in Goethe's poem about his Gingko tree. My late wife smuggled a cutting of Goethe's tree home to Cumbria. That gingko tree now grows upon her grave. Das Lied von der Erde is the symphonic sequence by the Austrian composer, Gustav Mahler (1860–1911). Tianmushan in eastern China is one habitat of the Gingko tree – Gingko biloba – where this pre-Ice Age tree grows wild.

Michael Geoffrey Baron - Biography

Michael Geoffrey Baron was born in London on Christmas Day, 1928. He was educated at Westminster School and Trinity College Cambridge. He endured working as a solicitor in the City of London, and Twickenham from 1956 to 1991. He then moved to Cumbria and worked in Whitehaven until 1994.

He is the father of an autistic son and co-founder of the National Autistic Society for which he was awarded an MBE in 1980.

In Cumbria he organized a poetry competition and initiated the Words by the Water literary festival held annually in Keswick. He was a board member of New Writing North and the Cumbria Poets Workshop.

He has edited and co-edited several anthologies including *On a Bat's Wing* and *The Night Shift* (Five Leaves Press) and *The Cockermouth Poets*. He self-published his first collection, *More than a Man in a Boat* in 2005.

The Gingko Tree and Other Poems is his first commercially published collection.

Palewell Press

Palewell Press is an independent publisher handling poetry, fiction and non-fiction with a focus on books that foster Justice, Equality and Sustainability.

The Editor can be reached on enquiries@palewellpress.co.uk

www.ingramcontent.com/pod-product-compliance
Lightning Source LLC
Chambersburg PA
CBHW040545170726
48295CB00012B/602